# HOOEY HIGGINS
## and the
# Awards
## of
# Awesomeness

For the Hooeys and Samanthas
of Kilmersdon Primary School
with love
S.V.

For Dad xxx
E.D.

# Hooey Higgins
## and the
# Awards
### of
## Awesomeness

## STEVE VOAKE

### illustrated by Emma Dodson

**WALKER
BOOKS**

This is a work of fiction. Names, characters, places and incidents are either products of the author's imagination or, if real, used fictitiously. All statements, activities, stunts, descriptions, information and material of any other kind contained herein are included for entertainment purposes only and should not be relied on for accuracy or replicated as they may result in injury.

First published 2013 by Walker Books Ltd
87 Vauxhall Walk, London SE11 5HJ

2 4 6 8 10 9 7 5 3 1

Text © 2013 Steve Voake
Illustrations © 2013 Emma Dodson

This book has been typeset in StempelSchneidler and EDodson

Printed and bound in Great Britain
by Clays Ltd, St Ives plc

British Library Cataloguing in Publication Data:
a catalogue record for this book is available from the British Library

ISBN 978-1-4063-3430-2

www.walker.co.uk

# CONTENTS

# TRAGIC TWIG

"If you actually did that, they'd take you away," said Twig when Miss Troutson had finished thumping out the chords to "One More Step Along the Way I Go". "Stick you in a straitjacket and lock you in a rubber room."

"What *are* you talking about?" asked Hooey.

"That bit in the song where it tells you to 'leap and sing in all you do'. It'd be absolute chaos."

"It's just a song, Twig."

"Even so. They obviously haven't thought it through."

"Shush!" hissed Miss Troutson, glaring at them over the piano. "Stop talking!"

*"See what I mean?"* whispered Twig. *"If I leapt and sang now she'd probably run me over with her piano."*

"Excuse me," said Mr Croft, the headteacher, standing at the front of the hall and glaring at a group of infants who were making faces at the row behind. "I am *waiting for quiet.*"

This information had no effect at all on the infants. If anything, it made them more restless. Some stuck pencils up their noses. Others coughed until their eyes watered. Some even hooked their fingers in their mouths, stretching them out into

shapes that, until now, scientists might have thought impossible.

CLASS ONE!

shouted Mr Croft. "Would you *kindly* PAY ATTENTION!"

At the sound of his voice the infants jumped into the air and landed on the hall floor with a soft *fluump*. Then they sat up straight and put their fingers to their lips, like tiny angels sent from heaven to demonstrate the importance of good behaviour.

"I should think so too," said Mr Croft.

*"They're gonna cop it later,"* whispered Twig as Miss Marshall folded her arms and glared at them. *"She'll bang 'em up in the Home Corner with a bottle of milk and a manky maths book."*

Hooey grinned. *"Is that what happened to you when you ate all the plasticine?"*

*"It wasn't my fault,"* whispered Twig. *"Someone had made a hot dog out of it."* He looked thoughtful for a moment. *"Tasted pretty good actually."*

"**Good morning, everyone,**" said Mr Croft. "**Good morning, Mr Croft,**" replied everyone except Miss Troutson, who was filing her nails with the edge of a pencil sharpener.

"This morning we are going to see who has been achieving wonderful things," said Mr Croft. "Those people will be awarded a special certificate."

I wanna speshy stiff-cut,

said Basbo, colouring in his knuckles with a red glitter pen. "Speshy stiff-cut for blappin' 'im inna bloonies."

"Who did he blap in the bloonies?" whispered Twig.

"Timothy Mimsy," hissed Hooey. "He showed Basbo a book on gorillas and asked if he recognized any of his family."

"He should get a certificate for bravery," replied Twig.

Mr Croft opened his folder and ran his finger down the list.

"And the first award goes to Maisy Tinkerton for tidying up the classroom so beautifully at the end of every lesson."

"Tidying up the classroom?!" exclaimed Ricky Mears. "Well, I blew my nose the other day. Maybe I'll get one too."

"Three, four," said Wayne Burkett, counting on his fingers.

As Maisy Tinkerton got up to collect her certificate, Basbo whacked Ricky Mears round the head and sent him squawking into the aisle.

"No stiff-cut for nosey-blow," he growled. "Stiff-cut for blooney-blap only."

14

"Ricky Mears," hissed Miss Troutson, glowering at him over the top of her piano, "get back into line you silly, *silly* boy."

"I always get the blame," said Ricky, rubbing the side of his head. "Snot fair."

"I'm not going to *that*," said Wayne. "Sounds disgusting."

"I'll tell you what's not fair," said Twig as Sarah-Jane Silverton collected her Worker of the Week Award for the seventeenth time in a row. "Me not getting a certificate."

I never win.

"Stick an 'e' on the end and you always do," said Ricky Mears. "Wine, I mean. Ha!"

"That's the wrong sort of 'wine'," said Samantha. "You mean 'whine' spelt with an 'h'—"

"And the winner of this week's Spelling Award is ... Samantha Curbitt," announced Mr Croft.

"Bye, losers," said Samantha. "I've got an award to collect. Or, should I say, an A-W-A-R-D."

"See?" said Twig. "Everyone but me."

Twig had a point. Yasmin Boothroyd was averaging several certificates a week. Sarah-Jane Silverton had won so many that her parents had been forced to build an extension to display them all. Even Hooey had somehow managed to win one for "Artistic Expression". He had been surprised because it was supposed to have been a painting of his grandma, and the headteacher had congratulated him on his lively interpretation of a cat.

"I haven't got *any* certificates," said Twig as he watched the teaching assistants carry Sarah-Jane's awards out of Assembly. "Not a single one."

"How desperately tragic," said Yasmin, pressing her hand against her forehead.

Twig frowned. "What does 'tragic' mean?"

"It refers to a tragedy," said Miss Troutson, "which is a sad, unhappy event. Or in some cases," she added, casting her eye along the line of children, "a whole series of them."

"There you go then," said Twig.

My life in a nutshell.

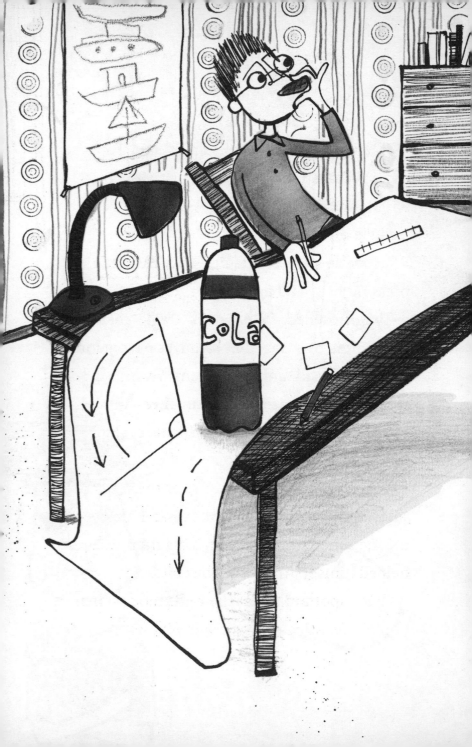

# INVISIBLE INVENTIONS

Will was upstairs inventing things when Hooey got home. A roll of wallpaper was stretched across his desk, weighted down with a bottle of cola at one end and a packet of digestives at the other.

"Hungry, Will?" asked Hooey as Will brushed the crumbs from his diagram and helped himself to another biscuit.

"It's important to eat the right foods when you're inventing things," said Will.

"I thought that was supposed to be fruit and vegetables," said Hooey.

Will took a swig of cola and burped. "Fruit and veg is fine for the everyday stuff," he said, "but inventions need extra fizz."

Hooey peered over Will's shoulder and saw that he had drawn a picture of an empty beach. Around the outside, in separate boxes, he had drawn a video camera, some TV screens and a duffel coat.

"It's an invisibility device," Will explained. "As you can see, the boy has completely disappeared."

"That's because you haven't drawn him," said Hooey.

"Ah, but *why* haven't I drawn him?"

Hooey thought for a moment. "Couldn't be bothered?"

Will sighed. "No, Hooey. The reason I haven't drawn him is that I don't *need* to draw him. And the reason I don't need to draw him is because he's invisible. See?"

"No."

"Exactly."

Hooey was confused. "But how did he get to be invisible?"

"Simple," said Will. "The TV screens are glued to the front of his duffel coat. All he has to do is put the coat on and there you have it: The Duffel Coat of Invisibility."

"Or The Duffel Coat of When Baboons Attack," said Hooey.

"They won't be showing *When Baboons Attack*," said Will. "There's a camera on the back of his coat which films whatever's behind him. If he's standing in front of a forest, the camera films the forest and shows it on the TV screens. If he's standing in front of the sea, as in this case, then it shows pictures of that."

Hooey's brain felt like one of those complicated locks where you need all the different parts to slot into place before you can open the door.

"So people looking at him won't actually see him at all," Will explained. "All they'll see is the sea,

which will make him invisible!

said Hooey as the last bit of information clicked into place.

"That's genius, Will! Shall we make it?"

"Slight problem there," said Will. "I had
a trial run with Dad's video camera and
the TV."

Hooey looked around the room.

"Where *is* the TV?"

"Let's just say some of my ideas are way
ahead of the available technology," said Will.
"And we probably won't be watching TV
for a while."

"No worries," said
Hooey. "I've got loads to
do anyway. In fact, I'm
definitely going to need
your brainpower."

"Best have another
digestive then,"
said Will, offering
Hooey the packet.
"What's up?"

"What's down, more like," said Hooey. "It's Twig…"

"Fallen down a well, has he?" asked Will, reaching for a new pencil. "Tell me how deep it is and I'll do a few calculations."

"He hasn't fallen down any wells," said Hooey. "I just mean he's down, as in a bit fed up."

Will nodded. "Basbo still trying to kill him, then?"

"It's not just that. He's fed up because he never gets a certificate in Assembly. On the way home he said, '*The milkmaid's lot is better than mine, and her life merrier.*'"

Will raised an eyebrow. "Gone mad, has he?"

"No, that was from some film he watched with his nan. But he's pretty fed up about the certificates."

"What does he want one for?" asked Will,

switching on his computer. "Winning Wimbledon? Saving the world? You name it and I'll print it."

"We can't give him one just like that," said Hooey. "He needs to feel he's earned it."

"We'll charge him then. Fifty pence plus expenses."

"I was thinking of finding something he can do well," said Hooey. "Something he could actually win an award for, fair and square."

"We're still talking about Twig, right?"

"Right."

Will picked up the bottle of cola. "In that case," he said,

we're going to need plenty of fizz.

# SEAWEED SURPRISE

"We need to come up
with a fancy name,"
said Hooey after they
had thought of some
things Twig might be
good at. "How about:
**The Badges
of Brilliance?**"

Will shook his head.
"Blew up the badge-
making kit."

27

"Oh, OK. How about... The Awards of Awesomeness?"

"Not bad," said Will. "In fact, you could give yourself a special award for thinking of it."

"Thanks!" said Hooey.

He wrote:

MAKE SPECIAL AWARD
FOR HOOEY.

"OK, here's what we've got," said Will. "Award of Awesomeness Number One: Making the World a Greener Place."

"That almost sounds like a real one," said Hooey. "This must be really good stuff," he added, finishing off the cola.

"What have you got for Number Two?" asked Will. Hooey looked at his piece of paper: "The Award of Awesomeness for Man of the Match."

"Shouldn't that be Man or Woman of the Match?" asked Will.

"Twig's not a woman," said Hooey. "In spite of what Ricky Mears says."

"I know that," said Will, "but we have to make sure that the awards are open to everyone, otherwise it's not fair."

Hooey looked at the empty bottle.

"In that case, we definitely need more cola."

Leaving Will to work on the certificates, Hooey decided to find Dingbat and take him for a walk to the sweetshop.

"Someone
thrown the dog
away?" asked Grandma as
Hooey dragged Dingbat out of the bin.

"I think he was after last night's dinner,"
said Hooey, wiping Dingbat's face with an
old dishcloth.

"You're thinking of *Britain's Got Talent,*"
said Grandma. "That was after last night's
dinner. I remember because there was a dog
on that too. Don't think he was in a bin,
though."

"Anyway..." said Hooey. "The thing is, I'm just off to the sweetshop. Would you like anything, Grandma?"

"I'd like Vera next door to shut up about her Cookery Club," said Grandma.

"Lemon bon-bons?" suggested Hooey.

"Get me **a giant gobstopper,**" said Grandma. "I'm telling you, if Vera mentions her coq au vin one more time I'm going to whop her over the head with it."

"Maybe I'll get several then," said Hooey.

\* \* \*

As Hooey opened the door to the
sweetshop, Mr Danson put down his copy
of **NOUGAT NEWS** and gave the Crunchies a
quick polish with his sleeve.

"The usual, is it?" he asked.

Two Crunchies and a
couple of Sherbet Fountains?

"Thanks, Mr Danson," said Hooey.

"I'm also going to need a bottle of cola and a bag of gobstoppers."

"My, my, we are splashing out," said Mr Danson, running his finger along the line of sweet jars. "Special occasion, is it?"

"Sort of," said Hooey. "The gobstoppers are for my grandma's friend and the cola is to help us think of ways to win awards."

"Awards?" echoed Mr Danson, shaking some gobstoppers into a bag. "What kind of awards?"

"Awesome ones mainly," said Hooey.
He thought for a moment. "I don't suppose
you'd be interested in presenting one for us,
would you?"

Me?

replied Mr Danson.
"Present an award?"
 "Yes," said Hooey.
"All you'd need
to do is judge
the winner and then give them a Crunchie
or something. He thought for a moment.
"We could call it ... The Derek Danson
Award of Awesomeness for
Fabulous Footballing."
 "The Derek Danson Award,"
repeated Mr Danson, leaning on the dolly
mixtures and wiping his eyes with an
embroidered hanky.

"I should be honoured," he announced, holding up a bar of chocolate, "to present the winner with my ROYAL BOUNTY."

\* \* \*

As Hooey walked
Dingbat back along the seafront he
saw Twig standing by the water's edge
in a pair of swimming trunks. He was
scooping grease out of an oven tray
and rubbing it over his chest.

"Twig," said Hooey, "what are
you doing?"

Rubbing
chicken fat
into my chest,

said Twig. "When I've
finished doing that, I'm going
to rub it into my legs."

"Why don't you just bung it in the dishwasher like everyone else?"

"Because if I did that," replied Twig, "it wouldn't keep me warm while I swim the Channel."

"Hang on," said Hooey. "What do you mean, 'While I swim the Channel?'"

"It was on telly last night," said Twig. "This man rubbed grease all over himself and then swum to France. When he got there, everyone went nuts and started cheering like mad. So that's what I'm going to do. I'm going to swim the Channel."

"This wouldn't have anything to do with those certificates, would it?"

"**Certificates, shmertificates,**" said Twig. "I've *always* wanted to swim the Channel actually. I've just never had the right amount of chicken fat available."

"You've never had your Grade One swimming badge either," said Hooey. "Last time you tried to pick up a brick in the swimming pool, Miss Troutson had to fetch the lifeguard…"

"Who took the brick away before I could get it!" said Twig, lifting his leg and rubbing chicken fat between his toes. "Probably to build himself a little lifeguardy house or something."

Hooey offered Twig the bag of gobstoppers. "The point is, you can't swim to France if you haven't got your Grade One."

Twig stopped rubbing in chicken fat, took a gobstopper and looked at Hooey.

"Why? Won't they let me in?"

"It's not a case of not letting you in," said Hooey. "It's a case of you SINKING TO THE BOTTOM AND DROWNING YOURSELF DEAD."

"Ah, but that's where the chicken fat comes in," said Twig. "Same as it helps chickens float around in the sky, it will help me float to France."

"Twig, firstly, chickens don't float around in the sky. Secondly, they've never swum the Channel. And, thirdly, it's goose fat that swimmers use, not chicken fat."

Twig stared at the oven tray. He stared at his white, greasy legs. Then he lifted his head and stared at the figure of Samantha Curbitt, who was jogging across the sand towards them.

"Well this is awkward," he said, as Samantha approached. He wiped his hands on his trunks, put the tray behind his back and grinned.

"*Hello, Samantha,*" he said. "*What brings you out here on this lovely summer's day?*" Samantha looked at Hooey.

Is he all right?

"He had a bit of a run-in with a Sunday roast," said Hooey.

"Indeed I did," said Twig, producing
the oven tray from behind his back with
a flourish. "In fact, I was trying out one
of my new recipes. It's called *Twig's
Seaweed Surprise*."

He scampered across
to a rock pool, pulled out
a few strands
of seaweed
and plonked
them in
the middle
of the tray.
Popping the
gobstopper on top, he wiped
some chicken fat on it and kissed the tips of
his fingers.

"*The secret's in the sea salt,*" he whispered,
tapping the side of his nose and winking at
Samantha. "*Makes my saucy seafood sing.*"

"I think sometimes you should just STOP TALKING," said Hooey as Samantha jogged off up the beach.

"She must be vegetarian," said Twig, staring after her. "I don't suppose Mr Danson sells goose fat, does he?"

"Forget the goose fat, Twig. We're going to get you an award that will make those other certificates seem like something you get on the bottom of your shoe."

"What, rubber?"

"No. The other stuff."

"Grass?"

"No."

"Puddles."

"No. Listen, Twig. Will and I have come up with some new awards designed to make the world a greener, more footbally sort of place."

"**Shweet**," said Twig. "You reckon I could win one?"

"That all depends on how green and footbally you're feeling," said Hooey.

"At the moment," said Twig,

I feel like a dead chicken.

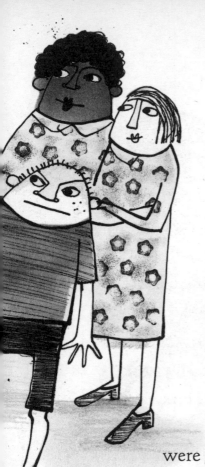

# TWIG'S TOP TRAINING

"There are two **AWARDS OF AWESOMENESS**," Will explained, peering over his clipboard at the children and dinner ladies who were gathered around him. "One is for **Making the World an Awesomely Greener Place**. The other is **The Derek Danson Awesome Award for Fabulous Footballing** against Grimbleton Primary tomorrow night."

"Who the heck's Mr Danson?" asked Ricky Mears.

Swaffagum, said Basbo, nodding his head furiously up and down. "Swaffagum and sherby widda chockystuffun crunkydunk."

"The sweetshop, you mean?" asked Ricky.

"Swaffagum, yarse," said Basbo, pushing Ricky into a rose bush. Will cleared his throat.

"I forgot to mention that Mr Bingley from **World of Wallpaper** is coming along after the football match to judge The Award of Awesomeness for Making the World a Greener Place."

*"Nice work, Will,"* whispered Hooey. *"Did you get any free wallpaper?"*

*"Twelve rolls,"* Will whispered back. *"Unused."*

*"Very nice."*

"But tomorrow's too soon!" complained Ricky, picking thorns out of his forehead. "I need time to practise my dribbling."

"I've seen you eat lunch," said Samantha, flicking up a tennis ball and bouncing it on her knees. "Trust me, you don't need any practice."

Think I might try out for the Fabulous Footballer Award,

said Mrs Parsons, the dinner lady. "I kicked a plate of spag bol straight out the window last Tuesday."

"Why?" asked Mrs Plunkett.

"Dishwasher was full. So I just—"

"Ladies, I think we're going a bit off message here," said Will.

"I can do this," said Twig, staring at the ground and clenching his fists. "I CAN DEFINITELY DO THIS!"

"No, you NOT doobery doodis!" shouted Basbo. "Stiffy-cut Basbo's, not Twonky-Faced Twiglet!"

Mrs Plunkett and all the other dinner ladies started laughing. "TWONKY-FACED TWIGLET!" they said, over and over, until Will asked for quiet.

"The main thing is that everyone does their best," he said. "It's not the winning that counts, it's the taking part."

"Yeah, right," said Twig. "Basbo can take part if he likes. But this Twonky-Faced Twiglet is going to *win*!"

Wayne looked at him and frowned. "Is it me," he said, "or can anyone else smell roast chicken?"

\* \* \*

Hooey and Twig went straight to Hooey's back garden after school. "OK, Twig," he said. "I want you to imagine you're **Wayne Rooney**."

"I'll try," said Twig, "but I can't do the accent, **like**. Ooh, wait. I think I just did."

"Never mind the accent, Twig. Just picture yourself owning the field."

"Like a farmer?"

"No, owning it, as in being in charge of it. You are the man, Twig. Go on, say it."

"You are the man."

"No, *you* are the man."

"That's what I said."

"No, you have to say 'I am the man'. Like that."

"I am the man."

"Say it like you *mean* it, Twig."

"I am the man."

"Louder."

"I am the man!"

"Who are you?"

"I am the man!"

"Yes, you are! Who are you?"

"I AM THE MAN!"

shouted Twig.

"I am the MAN!
I AM the MAN!
I AM THE MAN!"

Can you keep
it down a bit?

called Will, leaning out of the window. "I can't hear myself think."

"Sorry," said Hooey. "We were just trying out a few visualization techniques."

"OK, dial it down, Twig," said Hooey.

"I am the man," whispered Twig. "I am the man."

Hooey picked up the football and twirled it around on his finger.

"I want you to see this ball as your enemy, Twig."

"Why? I hardly know it."

"Because this ball is what's stopping you winning an **Award of Awesomeness**."

"It is?" said Twig.

"You have to show it who's boss," said Hooey. "You have to be boss of the ball. Let's start with a few crosses."

"Good idea," said Twig. "Keep the evil spirits away."

"Not those kinds of crosses," said Hooey, pushing Twig into position in front of the hedge. "This is the goal, OK?"

"Ooh, am I the goalie?"

"No, you're the striker. You're going to score goals."

GOALS!

cried Twig, clapping his hands together and jumping up and down. **"Oh, goody, goody, GOODY!"**

"You're the man, remember?" said Hooey. "Not the four year old."

Twig nodded.

**"I am the man,"** he said.

Hooey crossed the ball in low.
"DON'T THINK YOU
CAN MESS WITH ME,
BALL!" shouted Twig, pointing at the
ball as it went past. "If you don't do exactly
as I tell you then..."

"Don't yell at it, Twig," said Hooey.
"Just kick it in the goal."

"Right," said Twig. "Gotcha."

Hooey placed the ball
again. Twig was standing
with one leg on the
ground and the
other stretched out
behind him.

"Twig, what are you doing?"
"Getting ready for my kick,"
said Twig. "But you'd
better hurry up or I'm
going to fall over."

"Have you ever seen Wayne Rooney stand like that?"

"No. But then I've never seen him eat a Krispy Kreme doughnut either and I bet he loves 'em, the little rascal. Especially those ones with the sprinkly stuff on top."

Hooey sighed. "Twig, just stand normally. Wait until the ball comes and then kick it."

"Whatever you say," said Twig. "You're the boss."

"No, *you're* the boss," said Hooey. "Boss of the ball, remember?"

As he crossed the ball
again, Twig stepped forward,
shouting, "DIE, BALL!" and swung his
leg in the air. The ball bounced off his knee,
smacked him under the chin and knocked
him back into a pot of geraniums.

Dingbat trotted over and licked his face
until a fly flew up his nose and made him
sneeze.

"Maybe you should try heading it," said
Hooey.

He crossed the ball again. But as Twig watched it sail over his head, suddenly Grandma Higgins appeared from behind the runner beans, jumped in the air and nodded the ball into the hedge with a loud THWACK.

"One-nil Grandma," she said.

Thank you and goodnight.

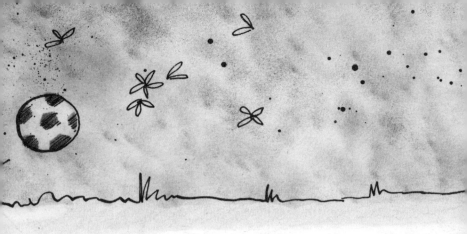

# HEDGES AND HEADERS

"NOW," said Grandma, pulling Twig to his feet and bouncing the ball off his forehead. "How does that feel?"

"Painful," said Twig.

"That's because you were just standing waiting for it," said Grandma. "You need to run at it full pelt and whack it with everything you've got. As my coach at Shrimpton Ladies used to say, if you stay in one place you're out of the race."

"He sounds quite annoying," said Will, appearing in the doorway.

"He was. But he couldn't half nut a ball." She ran back up the garden and shouted,

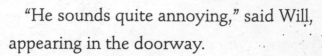

Let's have it, Hooey!

Hooey kicked in another cross and Grandma thundered towards it, heading it straight into the middle of the hedge.

Hooey looked at Will. "Maybe we should dress her up as Twig."

"She's too good," said Will.

"Run for it, boy!" shouted Grandma, holding the ball out in front of her. "Run like the wind!"

She tossed the ball into the air and Twig dived forward, sending it flying into the hedge.

"Goal!" shouted Hooey and Will, dancing around in a circle.

"Goal!" shouted Grandma, punching the air.

"Go-wo-woal!" shouted Twig, stretching his shirt over his head and running round the garden – then tripping over a garden gnome, screaming and falling into the hedge.

Grandma cupped a hand to her ear.
"That's what I like about the boy," she said.

"Not only does he score a scorcher, but he's still got enough energy to hum the theme from *Match of the Day*."

Will frowned.

"I don't think it's the theme from *Match of the Day*, Grandma."

"What is it then?" asked Hooey.

"I think it's **wasps**," said Will.

The humming grew louder.

Will and Hooey looked at one another.

Then Twig came
howling out of the
hedge, clutching his bottom
as an angry swarm of wasps
followed him across the garden.
"It was an accident!" he cried, the
wasps chasing him round and round
the flowerbeds. "I'll pay
for any damages!"

The wasps didn't
appear to be listening. Twig
hotfooted it into the house with
Hooey close behind. Unfortunately,
Will and Grandma had the same idea
and Hooey found himself squashed
in the middle of the doorway with Will
on one side and Grandma on the other.

Hooey was wondering if they would be
stuck there for ever when a wasp stung
Grandma on the bottom
and with
a cry of

she flew into the kitchen, sending
Twig tumbling over the hostess trolley.

Will stumbled in after her and Hooey slammed the door, wasps rattling against the glass like bullets from a machine gun.

"Well," sighed Will, "your heading wasn't so bad. If you can do a few of those tomorrow, you're definitely in with a chance."

"And Samantha will think I'm cool," said Twig.

"Let's not run before we can walk," said Hooey.

"I've been thinking about Mr Bingley judging the **Green Award** after the football match tomorrow," said Will.

"The thing is, he's got a wallpaper shop and every day he gets up, goes into work and is surrounded by the same old wallpaper. You see what I'm thinking?"

"He needs a new job," said Twig. "Ooh! Maybe we could get Mrs Parsons fired and make him a dinner lady."

Will looked at Twig. "Or," he said, "you could design some wallpaper with a green theme to it. That way you would qualify for the Green Award of Awesomeness *and* bring fresh excitement into Mr Bingley's life."

"Genius," said Hooey. "So, Twig, what artistic skills do you have?"

I can suck a crème caramel up my nose,

said Twig.

"Right," said Hooey. "That's not really artistic though, is it? That's just sucking stuff up your nose."

"It's performance art," said Twig.

"I don't think Mr Bingley's into that kind of thing," said Will. "He likes wallpaper, mainly."

"Also, I can chop courgettes," said Twig. "Chef-style. My nan showed me how."

"Again, not really art," said Will.

"They are green though," said Hooey. "Maybe he could do a collage with it."

"I'd need a lot of courgettes," said Twig, "what with all those doors and windows."

"Not a college, Twig. A *collage*. You know, where you stick stuff on bits of paper."

They went into the kitchen and found a courgette and a kitchen knife. Hooey pointed to the oven tray which Twig had left on the side with the chicken fat, seaweed and gobstopper still in it.

"Do it in there," he said, "so you don't make a mess. You can take it home with you later."

"No problemo," said Twig. He went SNICKETY-SNICK with the knife and suddenly there was a layer of sliced courgette lying neatly in the bottom of the tray.

"Not bad," said Hooey. "Not bad at all."

"Bananas are easier," said Twig, picking one from the fruit bowl and chopping it into the tray.

"I think you're supposed to peel them first," said Hooey.

"*It matters not,*" said Twig, holding up his hand. "*You have helped me on my path, and I thank you for it. But now I must prepare for battle alone. I may have the body of a weak and feeble woman, but I have the heart and stomach of a wotcha-ma-callit.*"

"*Why is he talking like that?*" whispered Will as Twig swept out of the kitchen and closed the front door behind him.

"Probably that film about Queen Elizabeth he watched with his nan," said Hooey.

"I think the drama's gone to his head."

"Well he's forgotten his oven tray," said Will. "I hope he can still come up with something."

"Whatever it is, it'll be original," said Hooey.

Will nodded.

That's what I'm afraid of,

he said.

# HOORAY FOR HOOEY

"What do you mean, I'm a sub?" said Twig as the rest of the team warmed up on the pitch. Basbo was sitting on the touchline eating a can of mushy peas and Mr Danson was perched on a camping chair with a clipboard in one hand and a Bounty bar in the other.

"How am I going to get to be the most Awesome Fabulous Footballer if I'm not even playing?"

"Relax," said Hooey. "He'll go on, won't he, Will?"

"All taken care of," said Will, patting his pocket. "Just leave it to me."

Evening boys,

said Mr Croft, the headteacher. He had been having trouble with *Angry Birds* on his computer and had decided to come out and watch the game for a bit. "I hear these new-fangled awards are your idea, Hooey. Is there something wrong with my certificates, perhaps?"

"It's not that," said Hooey. "We just spotted a gap in the market."

"Do what?"
said Mr Croft.

"What Hooey is trying to say," said Will, "is that your certificates are so wonderfully *inspiring* that he thought it would be a good idea if they could be applied to something extra-curricular."

Mr Croft put his hands behind his back. "Gap in the market, you say? Extra-curricular?"

"Makes the school look good," said Will. "And if the school looks good, then someone else looks good too, if you know what I mean."

Mr Croft raised an eyebrow and pointed to himself.

Will nodded.

Mr Croft smiled, shook Will's hand and then went back to *Angry Birds*.

75

"Nice work, Will," said Hooey, "but don't use up all your brainpower."

"Don't worry," said Will, "there's plenty left in the tank."

The visiting team from Grimbleton Primary were doing stretches and warm-up exercises in a neat circle. When the referee blew the whistle they all put their fists together, shouted,

GO, GRIMBLETON, GO!

and ran to
take up their
positions.

The Shrimpton team – who had been
warming up by pushing each other over
– slowly wandered into position too.
"Come along, come along," said the referee,
looking at his watch…

I want to
get home for
Question of Sport.

"They look pretty big," said Will as one of the Grimbleton boys stomped his way into the centre circle. "What do you think they feed them on?"

"Raw meat," said Hooey. "Probably have to catch it themselves."

"**We are so gonna get creamed,**" said Twig.

"That's not the attitude, Twig," said Will. "If you want this award, you've got to get out there and prove something."

"Yeah, prove I'm going to die," said Twig. "Hooey, they're calling you."

"**Oops,**" said Hooey, who had been so busy thinking about awards that he had forgotten he was playing.

"You're over on the right," said Samantha who was standing in the centre circle.

Hooey took up position opposite a dark-haired boy with the number seven on his shirt and a piece of cabbage in his teeth.

"Don't think you're getting past me," grunted the boy, "'cause you ain't."

"HOOEY!" shouted Samantha.

Hooey turned to see the ball bouncing across the grass towards him.

Uh-oh,

he said.

79

Hooey turned, pushed the ball through the number seven's legs and set off down the wing. A huge defender ran towards him but Hooey flicked the ball past him with the outside of his foot. He was about to cross the ball when something crunched into his legs and he skidded face first through the mud. When the whistle blew he looked up to see the number seven grinning down at him.

"Awww, diddumms," he said. "Did you trip over your laces?"

Hooey got up, expecting to be awarded a free kick, but then realized that the referee had blown the whistle because three of the other team were lying on the ground.

"They wuz all fussin an gettin me way annat," said Basbo. "So I's makin' 'em lie downgo sleepy-time."

"**THIS IS UNACCEPTABLE!**"
shouted the referee. He blew his whistle
again, shook his finger at Basbo and held up
a yellow card.

Basbo stared at the yellow card, nodded,
then took it from the referee.
"Fankoo," he said,
putting it in his pocket.

Basbo got
speshy stiff-cut.

The referee stared at him for a few
moments. Then he shrugged, blew the
whistle again and the other team took the
free kick.

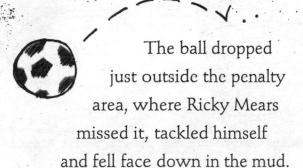

The ball dropped
just outside the penalty
area, where Ricky Mears
missed it, tackled himself
and fell face down in the mud.

**"I'LL SAVE IT! I'LL SAVE IT!"** shouted Wayne Burkett, rushing out and waving his arms, before tripping over Ricky and flopping down as if he'd just been shot.

The Grimbleton striker stepped over them both, waved at his friends and then hoofed the ball into the back of the net.

"**HOORAY!**" cried Grimbleton.
"WE ARE GRIMBLE!
WE ARE GREAT!
WE'RE GONNA BEAT YA
AND WE JUST CAN'T WAIT!"

Wayne slapped Ricky round the head, and
Basbo took the yellow card out of his pocket
and ate it.

"COME ON, SHRIMPTON!" shouted Samantha, picking the ball up and running back towards the centre circle. "We can do this!"

When the whistle blew, she passed the ball out to the left wing, where Yasmin Boothroyd was waiting in her new cashmere socks and bright pink boots. Yasmin trapped the ball under her foot and laid it back to Samantha, who spun past a defender and pushed it out wide to Hooey.

Hooey flipped it
past the number seven
and set off towards
goal. But when he
reached the edge
of the penalty
area someone
grabbed him by
the shirt. He struggled to keep
his balance. There was a loud
*thump*, a groan and then he was
free again. Neatly side-stepping
a tackle from a big
defender, Hooey
saw the goalie
running towards
him and chipped
the ball over
his head into the
back of the net.

"HOORAY FOR HOOEY!" shouted
Twig and Will, linking arms and dancing
along the touchline like a couple of
morris men.

Hooey turned to see the number seven lying on the ground with Basbo standing over him.

"Naughty-seven no take Hooey's shirt off," said Basbo, shaking his finger at the boy.

Hooey washiz shirt after, innit.

# PHONE CALLS AND FRIMPERTONS

At the start of the second half, Samantha
stole the ball from the centre forward and
passed it across to Hooey. Hooey could
see Mr Danson writing something on his
clipboard. He realized that if he wasn't
careful he might end up winning the award
himself, which wasn't part of the plan at all.

Taking the ball out to the wing he hissed: *"Will! I'm doing too well! What should I do?"*

"Do worse," said Will.

"I can't let the team down," said Hooey, pulling the ball back as the number seven tried to slidetackle him and went crunching into Twig on the sideline.

"THAT'S NOT FAIR!" shouted Twig as he crashed to the ground. "I WASN'T EVEN PLAYING!"

"We need to get Twig on," said Hooey, passing the ball back to Ricky Mears, who picked it up and started running down the wing with it.

"Oi!" shouted the referee. "Put that down!"

"Why?" said Ricky. "Jonny Wilkinson does it."

"I think we can probably afford to lose Ricky at this stage," said Hooey.

Will took out his mobile. "I'm onto it," he said.

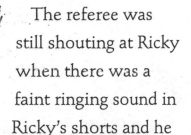

The referee was still shouting at Ricky when there was a faint ringing sound in Ricky's shorts and he took out his phone.

"Hello?" he said, holding up a finger to show the referee he needed some quiet. "Ricky here. What can I do for you?"

"Ricky, it's Mummy here," said Will in a high-pitched voice. "I'm just phoning to say the insurance has run out on your legs and you'd better not play any more until we get it renewed. OK, goodbye."

"He'll never believe that in a million years," said Twig.

"Sorry, got to go," said Ricky, walking towards the touchline and undoing his laces. "Insurance has run out on my legs."

"OK, Twig, you're on," said Hooey.

"When I float a cross in, just nail it like you did in the garden."

Twig nodded, high-fived Ricky and ran onto the field.

"Weirdest thing," said Ricky to Will. "I just found out my legs aren't insured."

"Reckon I could do you a deal," said Will. "Let's talk."

Back on the pitch the Grimbleton forward took a pass on his chest, flicked it up and volleyed it at Wayne, who had turned to wave at his mum. The first Wayne knew about it was when the ball thwacked him on the backside and sent him flying into the net.

"Thanks, Mum," he said, unhooking bits of the net from his teeth. "You could've warned me."

Meanwhile Samantha collected
the rebound and set off on a run up
the side of the pitch before hooking the
ball across to Hooey. Hooey held onto it
until the big defender stopped making faces
at Basbo and came running out towards him.
As Twig raced towards the penalty area,
Hooey crossed the ball high into the centre.

But just as Twig's head hit the ball, Basbo ran at the defender and the ball smacked him in the face before ricocheting off into the top corner of the goal.

Ow-ow, hurty-face, hurty-face!

cried Basbo, falling to his knees.

"GOAL!" shouted the referee, blowing his whistle and pointing to the centre spot.

"BASBO, YOU IDIOT!" shouted Twig. "YOU STOLE MY GOAL!"

Basbo lowered his hands and glared at Twig. The word "**Adidas**" was printed back to front across his forehead.

Basbo not niddiot! Twig banginna ballat Basbo! Basbo falloniz face annee flatniz frimpertons!

Hooey wasn't sure what Basbo's frimpertons were exactly, but he could tell by his face that he wasn't happy about them being flattened.

As the referee blew the whistle for kick-off, Wayne Burkett intercepted a pass and punted the ball to Twig. Twig was about to pass it to Samantha when he saw Basbo running across the pitch towards him with his fists clenched.

Twig screamed, jumped over the ball and ran off towards the other goal.

Twig was running so fast that several defenders thought he still had the ball and ran out to try to tackle him. Behind him, Basbo got angrier and faster, thundering through the defence in his efforts to get to Twig. It wasn't until Twig reached the goalkeeper, swerved around him and ran into the back of the net that the defenders realized he didn't have the ball after all.

Which was the same moment that Basbo scorched through the penalty area, thumped them out of the way and slammed into the back of the net with the ball still at his feet.

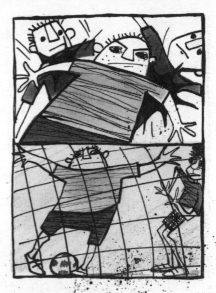

"**Careful!**" said Twig as Basbo let go of the net and fell to the ground. "You nearly had my eye out."

A big cheer went up and Samantha and Yasmin began dancing around the goal.

"**YOU DID IT!**" cried Yasmin as the referee blew the full time whistle.

"**You won the match for us!**" said Samantha.

"**You're a star!**"

Twig smiled and went bright red. "It was nothing really," he said. "I just saw the goal and thought: time for a bit of footballing magic—"

"**Not you, you great numpty**," said Samantha. "I was talking to Basbo."

"Basbo?" squeaked Twig. "But he was trying to kill me! All he did was—"

"Score the winning goal," said Samantha, pulling Basbo to his feet and patting him on the back. "I think we all know who's going to get the Award of Awesomeness for Fabulous Footballing now, don't we?"

Twig looked up and saw Mr Danson heading towards Basbo, a certificate in one hand and a Bounty bar in the other.

"Well, that's just brilliant," said Twig, sitting down in a patch of mud. "**Brilliant, brilliant, brilliant.**"

**Bree-yant,** agreed Basbo as Mr Danson handed him the certificate. Then he ate the Bounty bar, stuffed the certificate down his shorts and ran off to finish the rest of his mushy peas.

Twig stormed over to his schoolbag, opened his lunch box and took out a carton of crème caramel.

"Steady, Twig," said Hooey. "Don't do anything hasty."

"I'm not doing anything hasty," said Twig, ripping off the lid. "I'm just going to show Basbo and the world that there are some things only a true artist can do."

Then he walked over to where Basbo was finishing off his mushy peas and turned the crème caramel out onto his hand.

"Hey, Basbo. Want to see a magic trick?"

Basbo stared at the crème caramel and scratched his head. "Madjee trick wivva yum-yart?"

"It's not a yoghurt, it's a crème caramel, but whatever."

Twig looked at the small crowd that had gathered around to watch.

Now you see it,

he said, waving his hand ...

and now you don't.

He pressed his finger against one nostril and, with a loud **FLLOOOP,** the crème caramel disappeared up his nose.

"**Eeeyew, gross!**" cried Samantha as Twig showed the audience his empty hand, then bowed like an actor taking his curtain call.

"And that, ladies and gentlemen, is how it's done."

106

"Yum-yart gone," said Basbo, shaking his head as if he'd just seen a miracle.

"Yup," said Twig, dusting his hands together. "Guess that makes me the Nosey-wop King."

"Don't get carried away, Twig," warned Hooey. "Mr Bingley from the **World of Wallpaper** is in the hall waiting to judge the **Awesome Green Award**. And Sarah-Jane Silverton is about to do her presentation, so you'd better make yours a good one."

"Don't worry," said Twig, "I stayed up late and designed a special green machine that

will change people's lives for ever. I call it ...
The Twigmobile."

Hooey looked at Will.

Something tells
me we might need
a Plan C,

he said.

# WALLPAPER WINNER

When they got to the hall, Mr Bingley was sitting behind a lunch table and Sarah-Jane Silverton was standing in front of him holding a guitar.

"Mr Bingley," she said, "I was thinking that instead of making something that would simply add to the rubbish clogging up our planet, I would write you a song instead."

*"What's he ever done to her?"* asked Hooey.

*"You never know,"* whispered Will. *"It might be good."*

"I call it 'Skipping in the Sunshine With Mother Nature'," said Sarah-Jane.

*"Or not,"* said Will.

Sarah-Jane cleared her throat and began strumming a chord with her thumb.

"Skipping in the sunshine
What a lovely place to go.
That is the one time
I really, truly know
My car's not tootin'
And I'm not pollutin'
Or putting the boot in
To Mother Nature.
I won't make her muddy.
I'll keep her clean.
I'll go skipping in the sunshine
And keep her green."

"I think I'm going to be sick," said Ricky.

"Well, don't do it on Mother Nature," said Hooey. "She's got enough problems as it is."

Twig stood with a faraway look in his eyes, clapping his hands together and singing,

Skipping in the sunshine, skipping in the sunshine...

"Twig, get a grip," said Hooey. "You're on right after Ricky."

"Sorry," said Twig. "It's just so *catchy*."

"So was the plague," said Ricky.

As Sarah-Jane took a bow, Ricky picked up a carrier bag and went over to stand in front of Mr Bingley's table.

"Whenever you're ready," said Mr Bingley.

"This is the Green Award, right?" said Ricky.

Mr Bingley checked his piece of paper.

"It is," he said.

"In that case," said Ricky, "my plan is to sneak into hospital at night when everyone's asleep."

There were puzzled looks around the room. Ricky reached into his carrier bag and pulled out a roller and two pots of paint.

"While everyone else is sleeping," he explained, "I'll run around the hospital painting and painting, painting and painting, until at last all the walls are green. Then when the patients wake up they will have a greener ward, which will make them very happy. And then I will have a Green Award, which will make me very happy. And so we will all be very happy with our greener wards and Green Awards. And that is my very most excellent idea." He held out his hand. "Can I have my certificate now?"

"I think he's serious," said Will.

"Good job his mum doesn't pay for his education," said Hooey. "She'd be straight down here for a refund."

"That is certainly an *interesting* idea, young man," Mr Bingley was saying. "Does anyone else have a presentation?"

"I DO!" cried Twig enthusiastically. He fetched a flip chart from the back of the hall and wrote TWIG'S INVENTION at the top of the paper in green pen.

"Mr Bingley," he said. "Do you drive a car?"

"I do," said Mr Bingley.

"Did it cost a lot of money?"

"Quite a lot, yes."

"And then there's all that filthy smoke pouring out and polluting the environment."

Mr Bingley shifted uncomfortably in his seat. "What's your point exactly?"

"My point," said Twig, "is that I can save you money and make the world a cleaner, greener place. Interested?"

"Go on," said Mr Bingley.

"First thing you do is take the engine out of your car and replace it with pedals."

"Uh-oh," said Hooey.

"I know what you're thinking," said Twig. "You're thinking it would be too heavy. Which is why," he added, turning to the next page of the flip chart, "I would cut your car in half."

Mr Bingley looked as though he was about to cry.

"Why would you do that?" he asked.

"To save you money and keep you fit,"
said Twig. "But here's the really clever bit.
Not only would I cut it in half, but I would
also take off the roof and doors, and replace
the steering wheel with a metal rod. And,
hey presto, here it is ...

the
Twigmobile!

*"Are you thinking what I'm thinking?"*
whispered Will as everyone stared
at Twig's design.

*"I think I am,"* said Hooey. *"Twig's invented a bike. A bike with a car seat."*

But when he looked at Mr Bingley, he saw that he was nodding thoughtfully.

"Would it save me a lot of money?" asked Mr Bingley.

"Oh, yes," said Twig. "And think of all the extra wallpaper you could buy!"

"Hmm," said Mr Bingley. "Yes, indeed."

"I don't believe it," said Will. "I think Twig might actually win."

"Win?" asked Hooey. "By inventing a bicycle?"

"The Twigmobile is not a bicycle," said Twig. "It is the shape of things to come."

"I don't think it is," said Hooey. "I think the shape of things to come is wearing a T-shirt with KNUCKLE SANDWICH written on it. And it's heading your way."

Twig turned to see Basbo striding
across the hall with a can of mushy
peas clutched tightly in his fist.
He stopped by the flip chart,
pointed at Twig and
shouted:

Basbo dooda
disty-pee uppa
nosey-blow too!

"What's he talking about?" asked
Twig.

"Look," said Hooey.

And as everyone watched in
amazement, Basbo put a finger over
one nostril, tipped his head back
and snorted half a can of
mushy peas up the
other one.

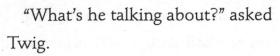

"Good grief!"
exclaimed Mr Bingley.
"What the—"

But before he had time to finish his sentence, Basbo staggered sideways, turned to face the flip chart and sneezed all over it.

AhhhhSHOOO!
AhhhhSHOOO!
Ahhhhhhhhhhhhhhhh...

The room
fell silent.
Twig stared at
the flip chart
and pressed
his hands to his
face in horror.
Not only was his
drawing splattered
with squashed,
mushy peas, but as
they slid down the
paper they seemed
to harden and set,
forming a lumpy,
green layer across
the page.

"Look what he's done to my design!"
shouted Twig. "LOOK WHAT HE'S
DONE!"

"Yes, look what he's done!" cried Mr Bingley. "Look what he's *done*!"

Hooey turned to see Mr Bingley clasping his hands together and beaming as if he had witnessed a miracle. "Bravo, young man! Bra-vo!"

"Huh?" said Hooey.

"Eh?" said Will.

"Don't you see?" cried Mr Bingley, pointing to the pea-spattered flip chart. "Woodchip is finished! Anaglypta is over! But this boy ... this boy has shown us the future! This uniquely textured design will be the start of my All-New Green Wallpaper Range!"

Taking a pen from his top pocket, Mr Bingley smiled, signed the certificate and held it out to Basbo.

"Here you are, young man. Or should I say ... young *genius*. I am delighted to announce that you are the worthy winner of the Award of Awesomeness for Making the World a Greener Place!"

Basbo stomped across the hall, snatched the certificate from Mr Bingley and stuffed it down his shorts with the other one. Then he ran over to Twig, shouted, "Basbo izza noo nosey-wop king and Twig izza crimbleshank cranker!" before crashing through the double doors and running off across the playground.

"What does that mean?" asked Will.

"It means," said Twig, sinking to the floor with his head in his hands, "that I can't play football, I've been outsnorted by Basbo, I'm never going to get an award

and my life officially SUCKS.

# TRIUMPHANT TWIG

"Never mind," said Hooey as they walked back home. "I think it's fish and chips tonight. You'll feel better with a good meal inside you."

"And there's treacle pudding for dessert," said Will.

"I guess," said Twig gloomily.

Shutting the front door behind them,
Twig sniffed the air and licked his lips. "That
does smell pretty good. But not like fish and
chips. Or treacle pudding for that matter."

"That's because it's neither of those
things," said Hooey's mum, coming down
the stairs. "Hello, Twig. You're staying
for tea, I hope?"

"Well, said Twig, "I—"

"Of course you are! You have to stay to tea, tonight of all nights!"

Hooey was confused.

"What do you mean, 'tonight of all nights'?"

"Aha," said Mum. "That'd be telling."

"What *is* for tea?"

"Wait and see," said Mum.

Will looked at Hooey, then at Twig.

"Does anyone have any idea what's going on?"

"None whatsoever," said Twig. "But then I never do."

Everyone sat down at the dining room table,
Will between Grandma and Grandpa, Hooey
next to Dad, and Mum next to Twig.

"So, Twig, dear, how did the football
match go?" asked Mum.

"Not well, I'm afraid," said Twig.

"**That's a shame,**" said Grandma and
winked at Grandpa.

"Never mind," said Grandpa. "Hooey
said you were going in for some sort
of **Green Award**. How did you
get on with that?"

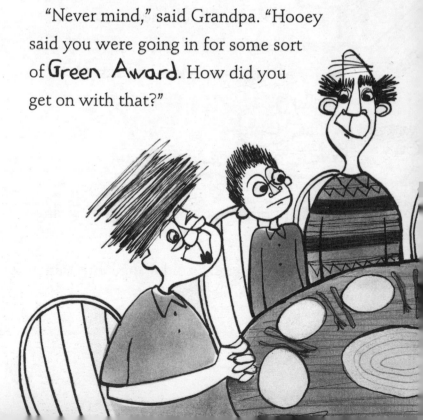

"Not well, I'm afraid," said Twig.

"**That's a shame**," said Dad and winked at Mum.

"Never mind," said Mum. "I expect you'll be wanting a bit of dinner."

She turned and winked at Grandma.

"I expect a bit of dinner will do him good, don't you?"

Grandma smiled. "I think it will," she said.

Hooey frowned. "Would someone *please* tell us what's going on?" he said.

"Certainly, dear," said Grandma.

She opened the door and, to Hooey's surprise, her friend Vera walked in, carrying a tray covered with silver baking foil. She placed it in the centre of the table and beamed at them.

"Go on then, Vera," said Grandma. "Tell them your news."

"Well," said Vera. "I've been going to Cookery Club for a few weeks now, and they were running a competition to see who could come up with the most original new recipe. So I entered and, to my surprise, I won. Everyone said mine was the most interesting dish they had ever tasted."

"Well done, Vera!" said Grandma. "Isn't that splendid news, everybody?"

Hooey was beginning to wonder if his whole family had gone completely barmy. They knew Twig had really wanted to win an award. But here they were, droning on about Vera and her Cookery Club Competition.

"Why don't you tell them the other news?" said Grandma.

"Shall I?" said Vera. "Righty-ho, then. The thing is, I couldn't accept the award for the recipe, because I sort of discovered it by accident..."

She removed the baking foil. Underneath it was a roast chicken in a baking tray, and surrounding the chicken were several strands of seaweed, some finely sliced banana and courgette and four multi-coloured gobstoppers.

"I call it: Banana Chicken à la Gobstop Seaweed."

That's my baking tray!

said Twig.

"It's not only your baking tray," said Vera, "it's your recipe too. We found it in the kitchen and I thought I'd give it a go. I have to say, it's quite the most unusual and exciting dish I've ever tried. And what's more, the Cookery Club agreed. Which is why," she added, reaching into her bag, "they have asked me to present you with their SPECIAL AWARD FOR MOST ORIGINAL RECIPE."

Twig's mouth fell open in surprise.

An award? For me?

he squeaked.

"For you," said Vera.

Everyone stood up and clapped and cheered, and although Twig kept saying, **"Oh, it was really nothing"** and **"This is so unexpected"** Hooey could see how happy he was.

When he thought no one was looking, Twig gave Hooey a thumbs up and whispered, **"We did it, Hooey. We did it!"**

But Hooey just shook his head and said, **"No, Twig. You did it!"**

139

When everyone had calmed down a bit, Vera said, "Now then *Mr Award Winner*, as it's your *award-winning recipe*, I think you should be the first to try it." She spooned some chicken onto Twig's plate.

Twig grinned.

"OK," he said. "Here goes."

He put a forkful in his mouth and chewed.

"**Oooh,**" he said.

"Yes?" said Vera.

"It's a little bit **chickeny** ...

it's a little bit **salty** ...

it's a tiny bit **seaweedy** ...

but mainly ...

it's ...

it's ...

**STEVE VOAKE** (also author of the Daisy Dawson series) was born in Midsomer Norton where he spent many years falling off walls, bikes and go-karts before he got older and realized he didn't bounce like he used to. When he was Headteacher of Kilmersdon School he tried to convince children that falling off walls, bikes and go-karts wasn't such a good idea, but no one really believed him. He now enjoys writing the Hooey Higgins stories and hasn't fallen off anything for over a week.

**EMMA DODSON** has always been inspired by silly stories and loves drawing scruffy little animals and children. She sometimes writes and illustrates her own silly stories – including *Badly Drawn Dog* and *Speckle the Spider*. As well as drawing and painting, Emma makes disgusting things for film and TV. If you've ever seen anyone on telly get a bucket of poo thrown on them or step in a pile of sick you can be fairly sure that she was responsible for making it. Emma also teaches Illustration at the University of Westminster where she gets to talk about more sensible things.